CRUMBLING CASTLE

For Felix
S.H.

For Sarah with love
H.C.

CRUMBLING CASTLE

by SARAH HAYES

illustrated by HELEN CRAIG

CANDLEWICK PRESS
CAMBRIDGE, MASSACHUSETTS

Text copyright © 1989 by Sarah Hayes
Illustrations copyright © 1989 by Helen Craig

First U.S. paperback edition 1994
First published in Great Britain in 1989 by
Walker Books Ltd., London.

Library of Congress Cataloging-in-Publication Data

Hayes, Sarah.
Crumbling castle / Sarah Hayes, Helen Craig.—1st U.S. ed.
"First published in Great Britain in 1989
by Walker Books Ltd., London"—T.p. verso.
Summary: Hoping to enjoy a quiet life working spells in
the basement of his new castle, Zeb the wizard finds
his life very unpeaceful thanks to Jason the crow
and the castle's other zany occupants.
ISBN 1-56402-108-4 (hardcover)
[1. Wizards—Fiction.   2. Magic—Fiction.
3. Crows—Fiction.   4. Castles—Fiction.]
I. Craig, Helen.   II. Title.
PZ7.H314873Cr   1992
[Fic]—dc20   91-58723

ISBN 1-56402-274-9 (paperback)

10 9 8 7 6 5 4 3 2 1

Printed in Great Britain

Candlewick Press
2067 Massachusetts Avenue
Cambridge, Massachusetts 02140

Contents

THE STONE CROW

When Crumbling Castle was new, it had a ballroom, a marble banquet hall, and four handsome bell towers at each corner. But almost as soon as it was finished, the castle started to fall down. Mysterious cracks appeared in the ceiling of the banquet hall. Tiles began to slip off the roof. During a thunderstorm one of the bell towers toppled over and went crashing down the mountainside. The ogre who lived in the castle began to hear noises. Sometimes it was a high, shrieking sort of noise. Sometimes it was a low groaning and rumbling under the floor. When the third bell tower fell, the ogre gave a great roar and fled down the mountainside.

After that no one wanted to live in Crumbling Castle, and it stood empty for a hundred years. Then a wizard moved in. He wasn't interested in bell towers or ballrooms or banquet halls. What the wizard Zebulum wanted was somewhere quiet to work, and the basement of Crumbling Castle seemed like the perfect place.

At this moment, however, things were not going well for Zeb. He was mixing spells, and a jar of tadpoles had disappeared. The lid of the toad bucket had come loose and toads were hopping around all over the place. One had climbed onto the table. Something green and sticky was dripping onto the floor. And Jason was talking.

That was nothing new, of course, because he was always talking. Jason was Zeb's crow—a sharp-eyed, argumentative kind of crow with glossy black feathers that stuck up in spikes however hard you brushed him. He was supposed to be the wizard's helper, but Zeb found him more of a nuisance than a help. There was one especially annoying thing about Jason: He insisted that he was not a crow at all, but a raven. And he never stopped talking about it. Even now, when he should have been herding the toads back to their bucket, Jason was standing on the table.

"Ravens have special powers," he was saying.

"So have wizards," said Zeb sternly. He had found the jar of tadpoles on a high shelf. Now he set it down with such a bang that three of the tadpoles splashed out onto the table. "And in any case, Jason," continued the wizard, "you are not a raven! You are a crow, an ordinary wizard's crow. And a very moth-eaten one at that."

Jason looked hurt.

"Ravens croak," said the wizard.

"Croak," said Jason.

Zeb was getting annoyed. He could not concentrate with Jason interrupting all the time. He pushed his glasses up his long nose and looked at the crow. "Ravens are huge birds with enormous, cruel beaks, and when they croak, everyone is terrified. Absolutely terrified!"

"Croak," said Jason again. He sounded like one of the toads.

Then the wizard began to mutter, and something very surprising happened. His face lost its furious expression. He became quite calm and pale. His nose grew long and sharp and shiny, and he began to turn all black and feathery. In less than a minute a large live raven stood on the table beside Jason. The bird was huge. It towered over the crow. Out of the corner of his eye poor Jason could see its great curved beak hovering above him.

"Cor-roak!" said the raven in a horrible voice that echoed around the room. Several mice ran to their holes. The tadpoles huddled together at the bottom of the jar. And the three that had escaped froze in their little puddle on the table. Jason shivered. "Cor-roak!" said the raven again, and a spider fell off the ceiling. Jason closed his eyes. He did not want to look at that dreadful beak.

"See what I mean," said Zeb in his ordinary voice. Jason opened his eyes. The raven was gone. The tadpoles were swimming around as usual. The spider was making her way back up to the ceiling. The mice were peeping out of their holes. Jason looked at the wizard. He was smiling a grim sort of smile. Jason fluffed out his feathers. "I could be a small raven," he said.

"I warn you, Jason," said the wizard. "One more word about ravens, and I will shut your beak for good." Jason looked at Zeb. He was wearing mismatched slippers and a battered old hat with a broken tip. His glasses had slipped down his nose. To most people he looked like a harmless old man. But Jason knew better, and at this moment he knew it would be wise to obey. Also, there was something in the wizard's black eyes that reminded him of the raven.

12

For a minute or two Jason was quiet. He hopped around the table gathering bits and pieces that his master had dropped. Zeb was not a tidy wizard, and soon Jason had made a large pile of trash. Among the things he collected were three tadpoles, a handful of dragon scales, one banded coral snakeskin, four small squishy things, a set of measuring spoons, and one toad. Jason did not exactly collect the toad. He pushed it along with his beak in the direction of the trash pile. The toad did not want to go that way. "Stupid creature," muttered Jason, and he nudged it off the edge of the table. The tadpoles were very squirmy, and it took Jason a long time to scoop them up in his beak and put them back in the jar. When he had finished, the table looked a great deal better—it was beginning to look very tidy. Jason was pleased with himself.

Zeb was humming. He had scraped the green sticky stuff off the floor and spooned it into his

13

copper mixing bowl. Jason flew up and settled himself on the wizard's shoulder. The mixture was beginning to fizz. "What's the spell for, master?" asked the crow.

"Oh, it's a sort of calming-down spell," said Zeb in an offhand way.

"For calming down storms?" asked Jason.

"Yes," replied Zeb absently, "things like that."

"And for cooling fires?" asked Jason. He was bored with being quiet.

"Yes, yes, for cooling fires, too," said Zeb. The mixture was giving off a sickly sweet smell.

Jason jumped up and down on the wizard's shoulder. He was getting very excited. "And for quelling waves," he squawked, "and for silencing thunder and stopping earthquakes and—"

"Silence!" roared the wizard.

At this point Jason should have known

14

better. But he lost his head. He flew down and pretended to read the spell book. "A potion for soothing the whirlwind," he read, "for quelling the storm, and for calming down mean old wizards!" Then he opened his beak and squawked with laughter. "Caw, caw, caw, for calming down mean old wizards," he cackled. "The raven has spoken," he added and laughed some more. He laughed so much he fell over and lay on his back with his eyes closed.

He did not see the wizard's face turn from pink to white. He did not hear the wizard mutter some words. He was still cackling when his feathers began to lose their shine and go dull. At the last moment he flapped his wings and gave a final squawk.

15

Then there was a strong smell of scorching and . . . silence. The wizard had turned Jason to stone!

"I warned you!" said Zeb. He set the stone crow on its feet and looked at it with satisfaction. "Jason," he said, "for the first time in your life you can do something really useful." He picked up the measuring spoons and hung them carefully on the stone beak. Then he turned the crow around and laid his spell book on the outspread stone wings.

"Now at last I can get on with my work," said Zeb. He sniffed the potion in the mixing bowl. The calming-down spell was beginning to work. He was already feeling much, much better.

All that day and the next the wizard worked hard at his spells. There were no interruptions. On the first day Zeb mixed a potion for turning lizards into dentists. On the second day he discovered a rhyme that made people's ears flap.

On the third day he learned a very long and difficult spell for turning things into chocolate. He ate a whole chocolate saucepan and then felt sick. On the fourth day Zeb tidied up the basement. He made a better lid for the toad bucket, and he wrote out new labels for all his jars. The stone crow sat on the table holding the measuring spoons in its beak and the book of spells on its wings. Things were very peaceful in Crumbling Castle.

On the fifth day Zeb decided to take a rest. He sat in his tidy basement and listened to the silence. And that was when the trouble started, for what Zeb heard was not silence at all.

What he heard first was a strange clattering, clunking noise; and then a steady *drip drip* dripping noise; and then he heard the sound of someone opening and closing doors; and once or twice he heard a little shriek coming from the bell tower. Worst of all, he heard a dreadful low rumbling noise that came from under the floor of the castle.

If Jason had been his normal talkative self, he would have told Zeb that all these noises were the ordinary everyday sounds of Crumbling Castle. It was just that Zeb had never heard them before. Stones were always falling off the walls of the castle. The wind often wailed around the lonely bell tower, and the basement had been leaking for as long as anyone could remember.

As for the terrifying rumbling under the floor, that was the sound of an underground river, or so people said. Hearing it now, Zeb thought it sounded more like a volcano about to erupt.

And as he listened to all the clunking and clattering and dripping and creaking and shrieking and rumbling, the wizard began to long for the familiar raucous tones of the talking crow. On the sixth day he made a decision. He lifted his book off the crow's wings and looked up the spell for turning things back from stone. The page was missing. Zeb tried reversing the spell he had used in the first place.

Rock and stone
Rock and stone
Turn yourself
To flesh and bone

Nothing happened. Zeb waved his arms and muttered some useful magic words. The stone crow sat stock still on the table and stared at him with its little stony eyes. "Drat the bird!" said Zeb. "He always was a stubborn creature." The wizard tried some more spells, but the stone crow remained a stone crow. Zeb was frantic. He shouted out every spell he could remember, even the long, difficult one

20

for turning things into chocolate. That one
worked all right, but now he had a chocolate
crow and what use was that?

21

Zeb heard a door creak behind him and a long crack appeared in the wall. Something boomed under the floor. The wizard pulled his hat down over his eyes.

"Come back, Jason," he moaned. "Please come back."

Immediately there was a smell of scorching and a sound of pillows being plumped up. Then someone squawked, "Behold the raven!"

Zeb pulled up his hat and there was Jason, as black and glossy and spiky feathered and talkative as always. "You're back!" he shouted. He tried to hug the crow, who quickly flew up onto his shoulder.

"Of course I'm not back!" said Jason. "I haven't been anywhere."

"How did I get you back?" asked the wizard. "What did I say?"

"I thought I heard you say 'please,' master," answered the crow. He flew down from the wizard's shoulder and started pecking around on the table. "I'm hungry. I feel as if I haven't eaten for a week."

"Six days, to be exact," murmured Zeb. He raised his arms and pointed to a little group of grasshoppers on the table. Then he recited the long and difficult spell for turning things into chocolate. Jason would have preferred the grasshoppers not to have been chocolate, but he gobbled them up just the same.

"Of course, ravens aren't all that fond of grasshoppers," he said, "even chocolate ones."

Zeb gave Jason a very peculiar look. The crow felt very uncomfortable. He hopped across the table and picked up the measuring spoons in his beak. He flew to a hook on the wall and hung them up. "That's where we keep them, master," he said. "You should know that."

"I should," said the wizard, "but I didn't."

"You couldn't do without me," said Jason.

"I don't suppose I could," said the wizard, and he smiled broadly.

Jason cocked his head to one side. "The crow has spoken," he said solemnly, and then he burst into a fit of squawking giggles. The wizard cackled loudly.

And Crumbling Castle went on clattering and clunking and dripping and creaking and shrieking and rumbling the way it had always done. And no one took any notice at all, not even the black beetles in the basement.

THE HAUNTING

The oldest inhabitant of Crumbling Castle was a little ghost who lived in the bell tower. She had been there every bit as long as the castle itself. She had seen the first cracks appear in the walls, and she had heard the first stones go tumbling down the mountainside. But the little ghost did not mind; she liked Crumbling Castle. And when the ogre left, the little ghost stayed on. There was no one to haunt any longer, but a large white owl came to live in the bell tower and kept her company. Life was pleasant but quiet.

Every night the owl would fly off into the darkness, and the little ghost would glide down from the tower.

She always took the same route—down the crumbling steps, through the cracked marble hall, across the ballroom floor, along a corridor, and then up the little winding stairs that led to the battlements. It had been years since she had met anyone in the castle, and the little ghost had almost forgotten what a good haunting felt like.

When the wizard arrived at the castle, with a line of bags and boxes bumping along behind him, the little ghost was overjoyed.

"At last," she cried, "someone new to haunt!"

"Who's new?" asked the owl, who was sitting on the great bell in the tower.

"The new owner of the castle, of course," said the ghost, "and that thing on his shoulder. I'm going to haunt them."

"You?" asked the owl.

"Of course, me," said the little ghost.

"There isn't anyone else, is there?"

"True," answered the owl. Then she swiveled her head around and closed her big yellow eyes. She never said much.

"I know I'm going to terrify them," said the little ghost.

"You do, do you?" hooted the owl. She opened both eyes very wide and stared at the little ghost. Then she spread her wings and took off. The great bell hummed faintly.

Some weeks later the little ghost was not so sure of herself. She had practiced wailing and shrieking. She had opened and closed creaking doors. She had hidden in cupboards and jumped out. She had glided along the battlements while the wizard was stargazing. She had done all the right things, but the wizard just did not seem to notice her.

"He's too busy arguing with that bird of his," she told the owl, "and when he does see me, he looks straight through me."

The owl blinked and said nothing.

"What am I going to do?" wailed the ghost.

"Do to who?" hooted the owl. Sometimes she could be very annoying.

The little ghost lost her temper. "The wizard, of course. That stupid, deaf, absentminded, nearsighted, unobservant old man in the bent hat!"

At that moment Jason flew up. "You must be talking about my master," he said. He landed on the bell with a thump.

The owl ruffled her feathers disdainfully. She looked at Jason through half-closed eyes. "Who are you?" she asked.

Jason drew himself up. "I am the raven Jason," he said solemnly, "familiar and aide to the wizard Zebulum."

"Raven indeed!" said the little ghost, who had been watching the two birds with interest. "You're nothing but a common crow!"

Jason's spiky feathers stood on end. His eyes started out of his head and he stared around him. Then he hopped in a circle, looking all around. The owl closed her eyes; crows were not of interest to her.

"If you want to know, *I* was talking about your master," said the little ghost.

Jason jumped at the sound of her voice.

He peered at the owl, who seemed to be fast asleep. He closed his own eyes. "Who's that talking?" he asked in a very small voice.

"The ghost of Crumbling Castle," replied the ghost. Then she did a little wail.

"Caw, caw," came Jason's raucous laugh. "If you're a ghost, where are you?"

The little ghost glided over to the bell and hovered next to Jason. "I'm here," she cooed.

Jason put out a wing. He felt something cold and damp. "I can feel you," he said, "but I can't see you. You must be one of those invisible ghosts."

"Not at all," said the ghost indignantly. "I'm the texture of clouds with trails of mist." The little ghost did not know it, but over the years she had begun to fade.

Jason peered hard. "Can't see a thing!" he said. Then a cloud passed over the sun, and

Jason caught the faint shadow of a small but definitely ghostly shape. Things like cobwebs trailed off the end of her skirts, and two gray smudges peered at him from the top. "You *are* a ghost!" he said, but the sun came out of the clouds, and all that was left was a vague outline that disappeared almost immediately. "You're gone again," he announced.

The little ghost was horrified. "No one in my family has ever become invisible before!" She glided over to the owl. "Why didn't you tell me?" she wailed. The owl woke up and blinked rapidly.

Jason looked sideways at the owl's yellow eyes. He did not want to stare. "Owls can't see much by day," he whispered to the ghost, "and I suppose you show up a little at night."

"I hope so," said the little ghost gloomily. "No wonder the wizard looks straight through me."

Jason put his head under his wing for a minute. That was his thinking position. "What makes ghosts fade?" he asked at last.

The ghost reeled off the answer: "A ghost will fade in the wrong place, at the wrong time, or in the wrong mood." Jason thought about that. A ruined castle was certainly the right place for a ghost. "I always wait till midnight," said the ghost. "We get these shivery feelings that tell us it's the right time."

"So you have the right place and the right time," said Jason. "But what about the right mood? What is the right mood for a ghost?"

The little ghost spoke as if repeating a lesson. "In order to frighten, a ghost must know fear. A frightened ghost is a fearsome ghost."

Jason hopped up and down on the great bell, which gave a hollow ring. He thought he knew the answer. "What are you afraid of?" he asked.

"Oh, lots of things," the ghost replied confidently. "When I came to the castle years ago, I was scared of everything—the booming and clunking, and the rats and the toads and the dripping; even my friend the owl."

"And now?" asked Jason sternly. "What are you afraid of now?"

The ghost thought hard. Then she spoke in a thin voice. "I see what you mean. I don't think I'm afraid of anything."

"Nothing at all?" asked Jason. "Not even ravens?"

"Ravens are just large crows!" scoffed the ghost. Jason fluffed out his feathers.

"Not skeletons?" he asked.

"What, afraid of old janglebones—not me!" said the ghost, and she gave a little hiccuping wail that Jason thought must be ghostly laughter.

"Not vampire bats or bottomless pits or creaking coffins or giant spiders?" asked Jason.

"Not a bit!" said the ghost firmly.

"Oh, dear," said Jason, "this is going to be harder than I thought."

The owl woke up and added, "Too true."

"You're not a lot of help," snapped Jason. Then he gathered himself together for flight. "I'm going to take a look in my master's books." He spread his wings and took off. "Back to the beetles in the basement," he called. Then he stopped in mid-flight.

The ghost had suddenly become very white and fluffy, and long streamers trailed out behind her. "What did you say?" she shrieked.

Jason swooped down to the tower again. "I said, 'Back to the beetles in the basement!' "

The ghost grew very large and thick and cloudy. Her eyes were black tunnels. Jason wasn't bothered by ghosts, but even he felt a sudden shudder. The ghost was wailing: "Not beetles," she moaned. "Not black beetles!"

So that was it, thought Jason. Everyone was afraid of something, and the little ghost was terrified of black beetles. Now Jason knew exactly what to do.

That afternoon Jason worked very hard in the wizard's basement. He told Zeb that the cracks in the floor needed filling in—two dragon's teeth had already been lost down there. The wizard mixed a special elastic filling material that would stretch if the cracks got any wider, and Jason spent several hours pushing in the filler with his beak. He couldn't talk much, so the wizard was able to work in peace. Zeb was delighted. Once or twice he wondered what Jason was planning, but he was too busy perfecting finger lightning to pay much attention.

Jason filled in all but one of the cracks in the floor. Then he waited. As the sun went down, a black beetle appeared out of the crack. Jason rapped the floor with his beak. "I want the biggest, blackest beetle you have," he said. "Pass it down the line."

More beetles came out of the crack and began whispering to one another. Soon the floor was thick with beetles, murmuring and buzzing and clicking away to each other. They were all ordinary small beetles, Jason noticed with disappointment. Then the crowd of beetles began to edge away from the crack. The clicking grew intense. Jason watched eagerly as a pair of huge feelers appeared. Then a perfectly enormous beetle emerged from the crack. It was ten times as big as the others.

Jason smoothed down his feathers. "Harken to the raven," he began. The beetles clicked and buzzed loudly. Jason started again. "Listen to the crow, I mean," he said hastily. The beetles were quiet. "If you do not do as I ask, I will seal the last crack in the floor and close your home forever."

The giant beetle raised a leg, which Jason thought was a good sign. "I shall need your help once a year," he continued, "but I mean you and your people no harm." The beetle waved its leg. Jason bent right down. He could see himself reflected hundreds of times in the huge beetle's eye. He tweaked his feathers into place. Then he outlined his plan.

A minute before midnight the little ghost felt her usual shivering feeling. "Time to go to work," she said. The moon was shining brightly, and the ghost was no more than a faint haze against the darkest part of the sky. She floated down from the bell tower, wailing gently. Halfway down, a lump of stone dislodged itself from the wall and went crashing down the steps. It made a tremendous noise in the silence, but the little ghost did not seem to hear it. She lingered in the marble hall and shrieked as horribly as she could. Anyone listening would have thought it was the wind whistling, for over the years the little ghost's voice had grown very faint.

Through the marble hall she went, across the ballroom where a large spider sat in a pool of moonlight, and into the long corridor. The wizard was nowhere around, but the little ghost opened and closed a few doors anyway because that was what she did every night. When she reached the battlements, she paused. The wizard was in his favorite position, leaning against the wall looking up at the sky. On fine nights he often stood there for an hour or more, gazing at the stars. Tonight, however, he threw out his hands and nodded happily as several small sparks came from his fingertips.

There were others besides the little ghost who were watching the wizard practice finger lightning. Up in the tower sat two birds, perched a little distance from each other on the great bell. Jason was trying not to laugh, and the owl, who had been out hunting, was sitting hunched up with closed eyes, paying no attention to what was going on below.

Somewhere a slate crashed to the ground. The castle shook slightly, and the little ghost began to glide toward the wizard. Jason peered down from the tower. The owl opened her eyes a slit. The shadowy outline of the ghost reached the wizard. Zeb shivered and pulled his cloak around his shoulders.

Then the little ghost saw the beetle.

Nestling in the bent tip of the wizard's hat, waving his feelers slightly, sat the largest, blackest, most terrifying beetle the ghost had ever seen. She screamed. She screamed a scream that tore across the sky and froze the water in the streams for miles around. The wizard fell backward. Rigid with terror, Jason watched from his perch on the bell. He saw the ghost grow thick and white. Then he saw the huge beetle open its wings and fly up over the battlements. The scream came again and again. The crow and the owl toppled off their perches, and the great bell swung. For the first time in a hundred years, the rusty clapper clanged. The bell rang hollowly. Jason and the owl began to plummet to the ground.

The ghost screamed again and again. The toads in the basement tried to hide under each other. The spider lay on her back in the pool of moonlight on the ballroom floor. The rats and mice and bats stopped squeaking. Only the giant beetle moved. It flew calmly on, down toward the basement. Its job was done.

As for the ghost, she was now a fearsome figure, and her white trails stretched the whole length of the battlements. Zeb opened his eyes. At first he thought a fog had come down over the castle. Then he saw two great black holes glaring at him, and the swirling trails of mist. "A phantom," he whispered, and fainted.

The ghost looked anxiously at the wizard's fallen hat. The beetle had gone. But the thought of it was enough to make her scream again and grow cloudy. Then she pulled herself together.

She swooped around and around, admiring the way her trails rippled over the walls. As her fear left her, she began to regain her normal size, but she was no longer just a hazy outline. Thick and white as cotton, she danced up the tower steps.

The ghost was filled with pride. No one had ever called her a phantom before. And no one had rung the great bell in living memory—how had she managed that? Altogether it had been a haunting to remember. She hoped someone had seen her. Perhaps the owl had been watching. The ghost floated up to the bell, but her friend was not there.

The owl was lying on the ground at the foot of the castle. Terrified by the ghost and deafened by the noise of the bell, the two birds had fallen senseless from the tower. A few yards from the ground, Jason realized what was happening. He spread his wings just in time and made a bumpy landing. The owl was not so lucky. She had fallen all the way. Jason stumbled over to her. The owl lay very still. Then the yellow eyes fluttered and opened. "Good for you," she hooted faintly.

"Yes, ravens certainly know a thing or two," said Jason. The owl opened her eyes very wide and stared hard at Jason. "And crows know even more," he added. Then he said quickly, "Let's fly back to the tower."

The owl struggled to her feet. "Too bruised," she said.

"We'll just have to walk," said Jason.

The wizard was recovering in his favorite chair when the two birds limped past him. He couldn't be sure, but he thought he heard them laughing.

ERUPTION

s time went by, Zeb felt more and more at home in Crumbling Castle. Every night he waved cheerfully at the little ghost as she floated along the battlements. And Jason became a good friend of the owl. She never said much, but Jason was happy to do the talking.

Only one thing worried the wizard and his crow. The creaks and groans from beneath the castle seemed to be getting louder. Sometimes the castle shook, and sometimes steam could be seen coming out of the cracks in the rock.

49

"Underground springs," Jason told his master, but Zeb did not believe him. The floor in the basement felt distinctly warm. Then the toads' pond in the dungeon dried up, and Zeb moved them up to the banquet hall, where the marble was nice and cool.

"Master," Jason said, "I don't like it."

Zeb was not listening. He was at a tricky point in a charm for invisibility that he was practicing on a spider. Either its legs disappeared, or its body, but never both together. Zeb repeated the charm and the spider vanished, all except for a pair of round red eyes that glared malevolently at the wizard.

"Master," Jason said again, "I don't like it at all."

"You're not meant to," said the wizard. "No one likes

spiders." He looked fondly at the red jewel eyes, which hung at the bottom of a thread. The eyes turned away, looked up, and started to climb rapidly toward the ceiling. When they reached the level of the window the eyes moved sideways and scuttled onto the sill. Then they slid over the window ledge and vanished.

Zeb was astonished. "That spider is a house spider!" he said.

"Castle spider," Jason said.

"She shouldn't be leaving!" said the wizard. "She never goes out. This is her home."

"Master," Jason shouted, flapping his wings and stamping. "Something is happening!"

At last the wizard began to pay attention.

Thick yellow smoke was now all around the castle. The floor was black with beetles streaming toward the steps that led up to the front door.

"Has it occurred to you, master," asked Jason, "that this castle might have been built on a—"

"Don't say it," shrieked the wizard.

"That might erupt at any minute," added Jason. The floor gave a huge lurch, and the room filled with acrid smoke. Zeb's eyes watered as he took down book after book, feverishly turning the pages. "Moving mountains, moving statues, moving staircases," he muttered. "Where can it be?"

"Master," said Jason, pecking at a feather out of place, "are you looking for something?"

"Pigeon brain!" shouted the wizard. "Here we are, sitting on a volcano, and you ask me if I'm looking for something."

Zeb glanced at his crow, who was busy preening. "Jason, do you know what has happened to the moving-house spell?"

Jason pecked at something on the floor. "I didn't think we'd be moving again, master," he said. "I gave it to some mice."

"Well, get it back," shrieked the wizard.

"They've shredded it," said Jason, "to make a nest."

The wizard was furious. He was preparing to turn Jason into something very nasty when a gigantic crack suddenly opened in the floor under his feet. The wizard almost fell in. He stepped back and raised his arms. The moving-house spell wasn't long, and he muttered what he could remember of it. The bottles and jars and saucepans and kettles and spoons began to

detach themselves from
the walls. The spilled liquids on the
table and floor slid back into their
containers, and the open books slammed
themselves shut with great clouds of dust.

"Follow me," ordered the wizard, and he
leapt up the stairs. But the objects did not
immediately obey their master. They clung
together in a floating bundle that jostled and
bumped at the foot of the stairs, unable to
get up.

"I don't think you got the spell quite right,
master," said Jason. But Zeb was at the top of
the steps and didn't hear. The crow poked and
kicked the huge swarm of objects, which
eventually clanked its way up the stairs and out
the door.

Outside the air was thick with smoke. The rocks were steaming, and the mountain was crawling with animals making their way down. There were rats and mice and spiders and wood lice and lizards and slow worms and some small banded snakes and a huge diamond-backed python no one had ever seen before. Clouds of bats hovered, and high in the sky Jason could see his friend the owl.

The wizard careered down the steps carved into the rock. The huge bundle of objects bumped along behind him, so close it threatened to mow him down. All of a sudden the wizard stopped. The bundle stopped too, and a jar of dried fish eggs smashed on the steps.

"The toads!" shouted Zeb. "You've forgotten the toads."

"Ravens never forget," Jason screeched.

"Crows do," said the wizard sternly. "And you are a crow."

"But master," said Jason, "all the other creatures have come down on their own."

"But not my toads," the wizard said. "Have you seen a single toad?"

"No, master," said Jason glumly.

The floor was rumbling ominously when Jason flew into the banquet hall. The toads were not there, nor were they anywhere else in the castle. While he was searching the battlements, Jason heard a faint shrieking from the bell tower. The little ghost was waving at him. He flew up to the tower, intending to use the owl's perch on the great bell. The bell, however, was completely covered in toads.

"I'm being invaded," wailed the little ghost.

"Trust them to go up instead of down," grumbled Jason. "Out!" he screeched. "And down!" The toads did not move, so Jason closed his beak and flipped one of them off the bell and onto the top step. Slowly it crawled onto the stair below. Jason flipped another, and then another. Soon the whole tribe was on the move. Jason flew above, directing stragglers.

The little ghost stayed in her tower, sad to see everyone leave the castle.

When they reached the ground floor, the toads began to hop faster; the hot flagstones were uncomfortable. As they passed the front door, a massive crack opened up right beside them. Jason thought he could see the glow of red-hot coals. The volcano could erupt at any moment! The toads were running now, falling over each other and hopping in all directions to get away.

Then Jason heard something, a noise coming from the crack by the front door. It sounded exactly like . . . like someone sniffing. Jason perched on a rock and listened. The toads tumbled past him; they knew where they were going now. It came again: a cloud of steam, and then, definitely, a sniff. It was louder this time and accompanied by something that sounded very much like a sob.

Jason cleared his throat. His mouth was dry, and his voice came out even hoarser than usual. "Is anyone there?" he asked.

A deep gravelly voice echoed out of the crack, "Anyone there?"

"The raven is here," said Jason solemnly. He could not think of what to say next.

There was silence, followed by another sniff and a sob, and a plume of smoke. As the smoke cleared, Jason saw something slithering toward him. He rose into the air, squawking with terror. Gradually the thing emerged. It was enormous and scaly and had huge talons. "A dragon!" gasped Jason.

"A what?" said the thing and burst into tears. Jason was almost blinded by steam and smoke, but he managed to fly down for a closer look. The thing's great arrowhead tail lashed nervously to and fro. Beside it Jason saw the remains of a massive leathery egg. He hopped over to the thing's head.

"You've just hatched," said Jason. "You're a baby dragon."

"Am I?" said the creature. It stopped crying, and some faint sparks came out of its mouth. "What do dragons do?"

"Oh," answered Jason, "they breathe fire and guard treasure and fly around—" Jason stopped.

"Oh, dear," he said.

"What's the matter?" asked the thing.

"You can't be a dragon," said Jason. "You don't have any wings."

Tears welled up in the creature's eyes. Then Jason noticed two lumps on either side of the jagged ridge running down the creature's back. They looked like balls of crumpled parchment. As he watched, the lumps began to unfold. In a minute or two, a pair of wings as thin and fragile as paper were spread out on the dragon's back.

"I can't fly with these," sniffed the dragon. "They're useless."

"I suppose you have to let them dry," Jason said reassuringly. The dragon sat very still, and gradually the tissue-paper wings began to thicken and darken until they were a deep

bronze color and the texture of leather. The dragon gave an experimental flap and rose a little way off the ground. "They work," it shouted. "I can fly." It circled around Jason's head, doing great swoops and loops and dives and glides. Then the dragon grazed its leg on a crag and fell to the ground, roaring with pain and fury. A great jet of flame shot out into the sky.

"You see," said Jason. "You can fly and breathe fire. Now all you need is a treasure hoard. You'll have to go out and find one."

"But how will I recognize it?' wailed the dragon. "I don't know what a treasure hoard is."

"You'll know it when you see it," said Jason. "It's a great pile of shiny precious objects."

"I'll be off then," said the dragon. It rather hoped Jason might come too. The raven, or whatever the spiky black bird was, had been so helpful.

But Jason had to get back to his master. "Good hunting," he cried as the dragon lifted into the air. It whooshed out a shower of sparks as a good-bye.

At the foot of the mountain the wizard sat down and put his head in his hands. He could not bear to watch the destruction of Crumbling Castle. And as he sat there, the great bundle that had followed him down the steps quietly floated past and glided off, unnoticed, into the darkness of the valley.

After a while Zeb stood up. He gazed thoughtfully at the mountain. The sparks and flames had gone. The volcano was certainly taking its time, and so was Jason. Zeb decided to start out without his bothersome crow. At that moment Jason flew up. "Tremendous news, master," he said. "The castle is safe."

The wizard exploded. "Of course it's not safe, you mangy clothes brush. It's about to be blown to bits."

Jason flapped his wings impatiently. "There isn't a volcano, master, only a dragon. A baby dragon, just hatched."

"Jason," said the wizard, "you have gone too far."

"It's true," the crow insisted, "a green and gold and red dragon. I've taught it to fly and breathe fire, and I've sent it off to find a treasure hoard."

But Zeb was not even listening. He was looking down at his feet, then back up the rock stairs, then out across the valley. "My things!" he shouted. "They're gone! My books, my cauldrons, my potions, my spells, my precious, precious things—they're all gone!" And it was true: The great bundle had completely vanished.

Jason immediately flew off across the valley. "Don't worry, master, they can't have gone too far." But an hour later he returned; the wizard's things were nowhere to be found. Zeb was still sitting at the bottom of the steps, absentmindedly stroking a toad that had hopped into his lap. "I will forget all my spells," he said in a broken voice. "And what is a wizard without magic?'

"I'm sure they'll turn up, master," said Jason, who wasn't sure at all.

"At least I still have the castle," said Zeb. "And the toads." Jason snorted as the wizard wearily got to his feet and began to climb back to the castle. About a hundred steps from the front door, the wizard heard a whirring noise above him. Probably the owl returning to her perch, he thought, and he did not look up. Farther down the steps Jason was toad-herding, and the toads were croaking far too loudly for him to hear anything else.

In the next few hours all but one of the inhabitants of Crumbling Castle returned home: The rats and the mice and the bats and the lizards and the wood lice and the beetles and the slow worms and the banded snakes—even the red-eyed spider, who was still invisible. "The rest of her will just have to stay invisible," said Zeb gloomily. The giant diamond-backed python did not return, which everyone was glad about. Tired though he was, Zeb did not go to bed. He spent the whole night leaning on the battlements, peering out across the dark valley. The owl was away half the night, searching for the runaway bundle. And Jason went out all the following day, and the next, and the next, each time flying farther and farther afield. Eventually even he lost hope. The wizard had abandoned the basement and now spent all his time in the ballroom, writing down every spell he could remember.

One day Jason went down to the basement to look for some toads that were missing. Halfway down the steps he stopped and peered into the gloom.

"Are you there?" he squawked.

"I certainly am," came the unexpected reply. Jason recognized that pebbly voice. He flew to the bottom of the steps, and there, all curled up and completely covering the basement floor, he found the baby dragon.

"Hello there," said Jason, trying to sound pleased. "Found your hoard, have you?"

He couldn't see any-thing except the dragon.

"It's here, it's here!" shouted the dragon. "I'm sitting on it. Isn't that what dragons do?"

"You're learning fast," said Jason. "How long have you been here?"

"Oh, days," said the dragon. "I was terribly lucky, you see, I found the hoard right away."

"Let's have a look," said Jason. He wasn't very interested in rings and coins and gold cups and the usual sort of things dragons collected, but he didn't want to be unkind. The baby dragon lifted itself up so that Jason could see what lay beneath it. Jason could not believe what he saw, for there on the floor of the basement were all the wizard's possessions—his bottles, jars, pots, pans, books, everything. The pile gave a lurch and the dragon slapped down his arrowhead tail on it.

"It keeps trying to get away," the dragon said. Then it looked at Jason, who was beginning to laugh. "It is a treasure hoard, isn't it? You did say a great pile of shiny precious objects, didn't you?"

But Jason only laughed louder. He laughed so hard he fell over. The dragon began to sniff, and the basement filled with steam.

"I know some of the things aren't all that shiny, but most of them are," the dragon said. Jason went on laughing. The dragon began to cry loudly. "You mean," it sobbed, "this isn't precious treasure at all?"

At that moment the wizard came down to see what all the commotion was about. He saw the dragon and he saw his crow; he saw his beloved spell book and his dented cauldron under the dragon's talons; and in a moment he understood everything. He flew down the steps and clasped the dragon around the neck.

"My things, my precious, precious things, you've found them!" he said to the dragon. "Do you know, that book is worth more to me than all the treasure in the world."

"It isn't shiny at all," sniffed the dragon.

"But it is precious," said Zeb. He leafed through the pages of the book, raised his hands, and said some words in a loud voice. Immediately all his possessions returned to their rightful places, except for the table and chairs, which hovered uncertainly over the dragon.

"You look a little cramped in here," said the wizard. "Would you prefer the banquet hall?"

The dragon breathed out a delighted shower of golden rain. "But what about my hoard?" it asked.

"There are some bits and pieces of gold and silver in the banquet hall," said Zeb. "Would you like those?" A cloud of stars burst out of the dragon's mouth.

And so it was settled. The dragon lived in the marble hall and became the official guardian of Crumbling Castle's treasure. No one really wanted the gold and silver knives and forks and candlesticks, but they were too polite to tell the dragon.

The mountain stopped rumbling and the castle stopped crumbling. And Jason found the missing toads, and for two whole weeks he was nice to them. After all it was they, in a roundabout way, who had brought back his master's treasure.

SARAH HAYES worked in publishing and then as a free-lance writer and editor before beginning her career as a children's book author. She has written nearly twenty books for children, including *The Cats of Tiffany Street, This Is the Bear, This Is the Bear and the Scary Night,* and *This Is the Bear and the Picnic Lunch.*

HELEN CRAIG worked as a commercial photographer for more than ten years before she began drawing and sculpting. Since her first children's book was published in 1970, she has illustrated more than thirty books for children, including Sarah Hayes's This Is the Bear books and the Angelina Ballerina books by Katharine Holabird, as well as her own retelling of *The Town Mouse and the Country Mouse.*